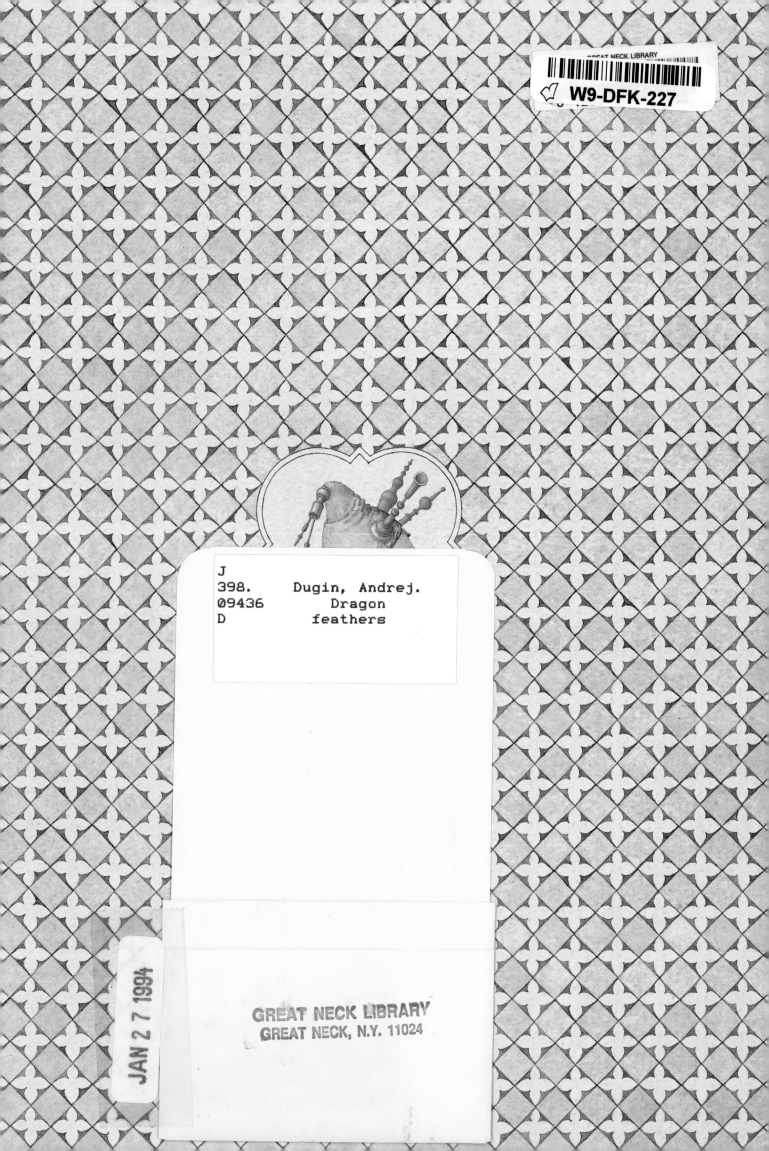

Dragon Feathers

Published in 1993 by Thomasson-Grant, Inc.,
One Morton Drive, Suite 500, Charlottesville,
Virginia 22903-6806

Copyright © 1993 by Verlag J.F. Schreiber GmbH,
P.O. 285, D-73703 Esslingen, Germany
All rights reserved. No part of this book may be
reproduced or transmitted in any form or by any
means without permission from the publisher.

First published in Germany by
Verlag J.F. Schreiber GmbH, Esslingen
American edition edited by Hoke Perkins

Printed and bound in Belgium

00 99 98 97 96 95 94 93   5 4 3 2 1

Library of Congress
Cataloging-in-Publication Data

Dugin, Andrej.
    [Drachenfedern. English]
    Dragon feathers / Andrej Dugin and Olga Dugina.
        p. cm.
    Summary : A poor woodcutter's son must pluck
three feathers from the wings of a terrible dragon to
win the hand of the innkeeper's daughter.
    ISBN 1-56566-047-1
    [1. Fairy tales. 2. Folklore—Austria.] I. Dugina,
Olga, ill. II. Title.
    PZ8.D885Dr   1993
    398.21—dc20
    [E]   93-8700
                                            CIP
                                            AC

Dragon Feathers

Andrej Dugin and Olga Dugina

Thomasson-Grant

CHARLOTTESVILLE, VIRGINIA

Once upon a time there was a rich innkeeper who had a beautiful daughter. In a hut next to the inn lived a poor woodcutter and his son, Henry. Henry was a sprightly young man, the most handsome lad in the village, and he was honest and hardworking. The boy was always good-humored and busy at some task or other, but whenever he saw Lucy, the innkeeper's daughter, he stopped whatever he was doing and could only stand and stare.

Now, Lucy was also heartsick for the woodcutter's son. Unfortunately, Henry was poor, and Lucy feared that if she asked her father for his blessing, he would refuse. But you never know until you try, and so the bold girl took her beloved before her father and asked if they could marry.

"You foolish girl," roared the innkeeper. And with a cruel laugh he turned to Henry and said, "The only way you can win my Lucy's hand is to go to the dragon of the forest, pull out three of his golden feathers, and bring them back to me."

Henry knew that the dragon was a great sorcerer who destroyed any human in his sight, but heartened by Lucy's bravery, he said he would face the beast. He set off at once for the dragon's castle, which he knew was hidden in a gloomy wood only a day's walk away.

Along the road Henry passed a cottage where a farmer sat crying and moaning, his head buried in his hands. "Why are you so sad?" Henry asked.

"My daughter has been ill for many years, and only one so wise as the dragon could help her, but—"

Henry interrupted, saying, "I'm on my way to the dragon's castle. Perhaps I can ask him what to do. I'll tell you what he says when I return."

The woodcutter's son continued on his way until he came to a wide green meadow, where he saw many people gathered around an apple tree. "Is this tree so beautiful that you all must stand and stare at it?" Henry asked.

A gentleman in the crowd answered: "The tree would certainly please us if it still dropped golden apples as it used to, but now it bears only thorns. If someone were brave enough to go and ask the dragon what has gone wrong, we would pay him handsomely."

"I will speak to the dragon," said Henry, and he set out again.

From the top of the next hill, Henry could see the dragon's palace shining in the distance, and he quickened his steps. He soon came to a broad river, where an old fisherman offered to take him across.

As Henry climbed into the small boat, the man began to weep.

"What makes you unhappy,•fisherman?" asked Henry.

"I've been forced to pole my boat back and forth across this wide river all my life, and I am•growing weary. Only the dragon can free me from my endless labor, but he takes no pity on me."

As Henry stepped from the ferry, he offered to speak to the dragon, and the fisherman promised him a great reward.

Leaving the river behind, the woodcutter's son entered the forest and began climbing a steep path. Soon he saw the walls of the dragon's palace glittering before him.

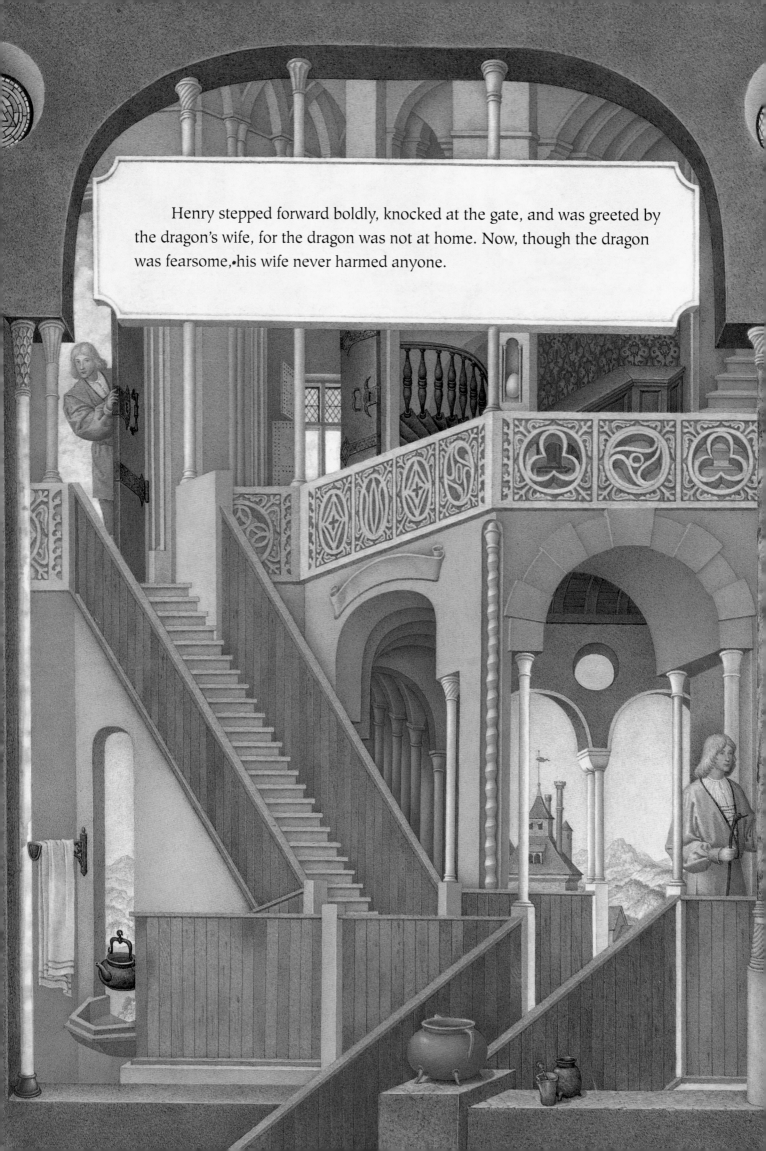

Henry stepped forward boldly, knocked at the gate, and was greeted by the dragon's wife, for the dragon was not at home. Now, though the dragon was fearsome, his wife never harmed anyone.

"How may I help you, kind sir?" she asked.

Henry explained his love for Lucy, the task set by her father, and the woes of the sick girl, the apple tree, and the fisherman.

"No human may speak with the dragon; he eats them all," replied the dragon's wife. "But come and hide under our bed, and keep your ears open. The things you wish to know, I will ask him," she said gently.

Late, late that night the dragon returned home. As soon as he entered
the palace, he stretched out his neck, peered all around, sniffed the air,
and roared, "I smell . . . I smell . . . a woodcutter's son."
"No, no, my dear," replied the dragon's wife, stroking his feathers and gazing up
at him. "No one has been here all day." The dragon slowly calmed down, and
as his wife murmured flattering words to him, he grew silent and contented.

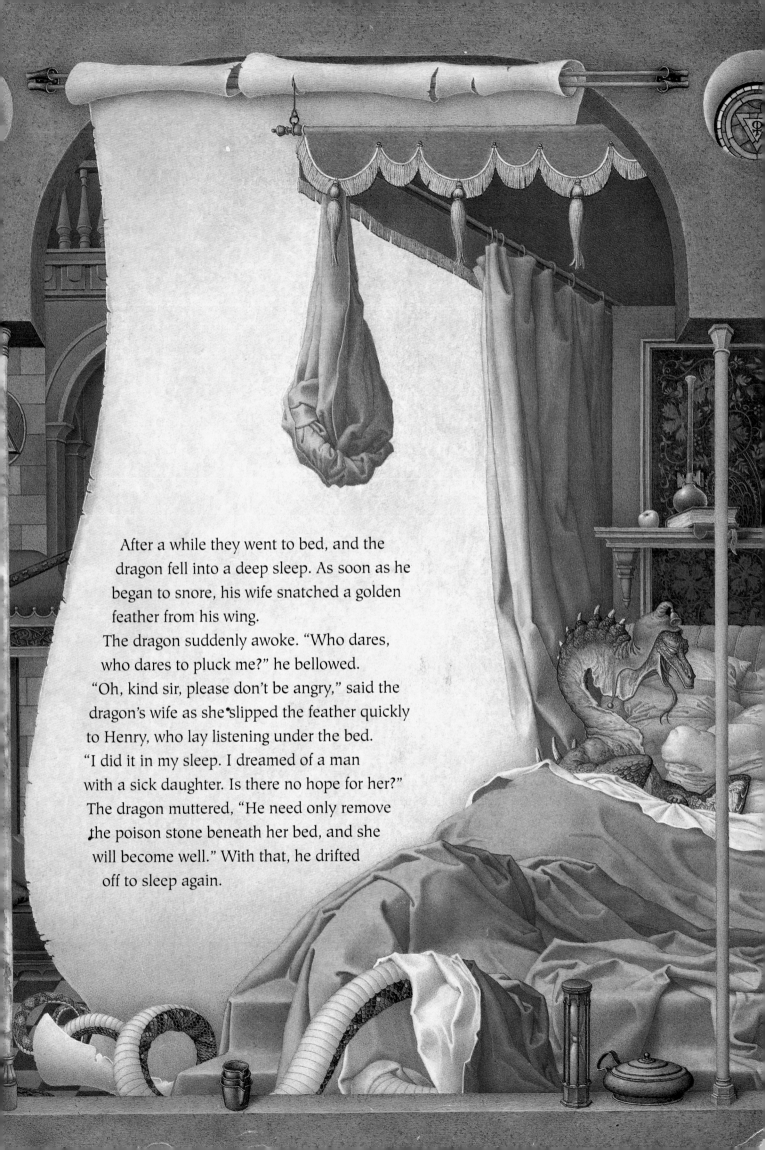

After a while they went to bed, and the
dragon fell into a deep sleep. As soon as he
began to snore, his wife snatched a golden
feather from his wing.

The dragon suddenly awoke. "Who dares,
who dares to pluck me?" he bellowed.

"Oh, kind sir, please don't be angry," said the
dragon's wife as she slipped the feather quickly
to Henry, who lay listening under the bed.
"I did it in my sleep. I dreamed of a man
with a sick daughter. Is there no hope for her?"
The dragon muttered, "He need only remove
the poison stone beneath her bed, and she
will become well." With that, he drifted
off to sleep again.

As soon as the dragon began to snore, his wife pulled out another feather and handed it to Henry.

"Who dares, who dares to pluck me?" roared the dragon.

"Lie still, my sweet husband. I had a dream about a tree that no longer bears golden apples. If only I knew how it might become fruitful again, I could sleep peacefully."

"A snake lies under the tree devouring the roots. It must be dug out and killed," said the dragon, and soon dropped off to sleep again.

Swiftly, the wife snatched out the third golden feather and dropped it to Henry. The dragon sat up in a rage, ready to spring from the bed. "Who dares, who dares to pluck me?" he screeched in a terrible high voice.

But his wife held him tight in her arms and said,
"Quiet, quiet, my dear. I dreamed of a fisherman who must
forever pole a ferry across a broad river."
"The silly fool may give the job to the first person who comes
to him, then run away a free man," the dragon snorted.
"Now, leave me in peace!"
As the dragon fell asleep, Henry crawled silently from
his hiding place, whispered his thanks to the dragon's wife,
and crept out of the castle.

Setting out for home, Henry soon reached
the ferry. The fisherman asked him hopefully
for news from the dragon. "Please take me
across the river first," said Henry.

As soon as they bumped against the far bank, Henry told the fisherman, "The next time someone comes along, put the pole in his hands, and he must take your place forever." So happy was the fisherman that he gave Henry all his money.

Henry made his way back to where the people stood around the barren apple tree. As soon as he told them of the snake, they dug it out and killed it, and immediately the tree began to bud and bear golden fruit again. The people were so joyous that they loaded Henry with gold and silver.

Upon reaching the farmer's cottage, Henry told him the dragon's words. When the man removed the poison stone, his daughter leapt from the bed with the bloom of health in her cheeks. The delighted father sent Henry on his way with a thousand thanks and a bag of coins.

Happiest of all was Lucy when she saw her dear Henry again. She gazed into her beloved's eyes as he told her his story, then took him by the hand to see her father. Henry gave the innkeeper the three golden feathers, and since the woodcutter's son was now far richer than he himself, Lucy's father agreed to their marriage.

"Where in the world did you get all this money?" asked the innkeeper.

"From the dragon in the dark forest," replied Henry. "The easiest way to get there is to take the ferry."

The innkeeper set out at once, but strange to say, he was never heard from again.

Henry and Lucy invited all the people of the village to their wedding party in the courtyard of the inn. Everyone feasted and danced, but the young lovers danced longest into the night.